True Ghost Stories and Hauntings

True Ghost Stories & Hauntings

Chilling Stories of Poltergeists, Unexplained
Phenomenon, and Haunted Houses

Volume IV

Simon B. Murik

True Ghost Stories and Hauntings

Chilling Stories of Poltergeists, Unexplained Phenomenon, and Haunted Houses

Volume IV

Simon B Murik

Published by:

Paranormal Publishing

www.ParanormalPublishing.net

ISBN: 978-0-9971185-3-7

Acknowledgements

A special thank you to all those who shared their experiences of the paranormal to make this collection of ghost stories and hauntings possible. Whether you believe in ghosts or are just curious about the other side, we sincerely hope you enjoy reading this book.

Names and places within the stories have been changed to protect the privacy of those who contributed to this book.

Contents

Introduction

True Ghost Stories and Hauntings, Volume IV is the fourth in the extremely popular series of books featuring true ghost stories and hauntings which have been collected, reviewed, and edited by Simon B. Murik. Simon is the son of a long line of mediums and sensitives originally from Eastern Europe. Many of the stories come from his own experiences while others have been contributed by family members and those who have shared their paranormal experiences with him.

If you enjoy ghost stories and reading about paranormal experiences, you will love this book. Get ready for a few chills and goosebumps as you read about haunted houses, poltergeists, and other unexplained phenomenon!

Be sure to check out Volumes I, II, and III of *True Ghost Stories and Hauntings* as well as other offerings from Paranormal Publishing at www.paranormalpublishing.com.

BONUS
Get 3 FREE ghost stories at
www.paranormalpublishing.com/ghoststories

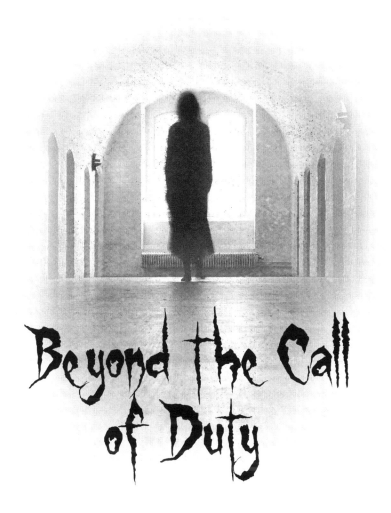

Beyond the Call of Duty

was never a believer in the supernatural. Let me just get that out of the way. I was raised to question everything. To me, there was always a logical explanation. Well, the story I'm about to tell you *has* a logical explanation. It's the logic itself that has me baffled.

My husband, Bryan, was stationed in Iraq during Operation Enduring Freedom. Our son, Matthew, was five at the time. I tried to explain to him as best as I could what Daddy did. He grasped it on a five-year-old level: The country that we lived in needed to be protected and Daddy's job was to do just that. Also, Daddy had to go away to do his job.

We got a boost around that time when the local paper did a story on the military men and women of our town who were stationed in the Middle East. There in black and white was a picture of Daddy and his entire company. Matthew used to look at the picture all the time. He was proud of his father. He'd look at the picture and try to pick him out of the crowd. He did it well—and often. I finally got the idea to clip the picture from the paper and put it in a frame next to Matthew's bed. It would be both the first and the last thing he'd see every day.

That night—I remember it was a particularly warm night in early June—I heard Matthew talking to someone in his room.

I poked my head in. "You're supposed to be going to sleep."

"I know," he said, "but I'm talking to my friend, Flapjack."

I smiled. "Flapjack, huh?" He was always conjuring up imaginary friends.

"Yeah. Flapjack wants to tell you something."

"Oh? And what does he want to tell me?"

He pointed to the framed picture of the military company. "He wants to tell you that Daddy is a good and brave man."

"Does he, now," I said. "Well you can tell Flapjack that I whole-heartedly agree. Now go to sleep."

About an hour later, just as I was getting ready for bed myself, I heard Matthew sobbing. I went into his room.

"Honey, what's wrong?"

He was inconsolable. Finally, he spoke through his sobs. "Flap … Jack … told me … something bad happened … to Daddy." He completely crumbled on the last word, drawing out the "y" through unending sobs.

I held him and whispered soft words to him.

Now, as a military wife, of course I had to deal with the prospect of something bad happening to Bryan. You had to be a realist. But I never had that talk with Matthew. I have to say it unnerved me. Perhaps he saw something about a soldier on TV and got the idea in his head that way.

I told him everything was going to be OK and rocked him in my arms. He fell asleep and that was that.

Thanks a lot, Flapjack! I thought as I tiptoed out of the room.

I read one time that kids will invent imaginary friends as an outlet for dealing with stressful situations. I remembered that fact that night, and it occurred to me that I'd never really considered just how much a jolt to poor Matthew's world it was for his father to leave him like that.

Overall, I think I'm a good mom, but that night I resolved to pay just a little more attention to my son's needs from then on. After all, we were both in this thing together. It was just us.

I didn't realize just how salient that fact was until the next morning, when I got a phone call telling me that Bryan had been killed in heavy action with the enemy.

I had no idea how to talk to Matthew about this. I myself was devastated. Beyond devastated. It's easy to write about it in retrospect, but I'm telling you, at the time, my entire world had gone black, and my heart was split in two.

I sat on the edge of my bed in near-complete denial. *This can't be happening.*

Matthew was calling me.

I composed myself as best as I could. I don't know how I did it.

When I opened his door, Matthew said, "Flapjack won't leave me alone."

That's just what I need, I thought. I really needed my son's imaginary friend to be telling him more upsetting things about his father. We had a very real thing right before us, and I was at a loss on how to deal with that one.

OK, so fast forward to about a month later. I enrolled Matthew in sessions with a child therapist who I hoped would be instrumental in helping him cope with the tragedy. The doctor told me that Matthew had a fruitful imagination, and that this would be beneficial.

"His tells me he meets with his friend Flapjack all the time," the doctor told me. "Only at night though. Do you hear him talking by himself?"

I told him I did. Every night.

The doctor nodded in apparent thought. "Hmm. The one thing that concerns me just a little bit is that he says Flapjack won't leave him alone. I pressed him on it but he won't elaborate. We'll keep an eye on him. I wouldn't worry about it so much."

"What do you think it means?"

"I believe it's a coping mechanism. He misses his father. By projecting onto Flapjack, Matthew is able to cope with the feelings of agitation and anger at his father leaving. For instance, he says his friend, Flapjack, won't leave him alone. This makes sense once we realize that Flapjack is merely a personification of Matthew's own feelings. His own feelings won't leave him alone. If we're able to help Matthew deal with these feelings constructively, I have a feeling Flapjack will go away."

It made sense. That is, until a few days later when Matthew came up to me and said, in a truly sad voice, that Flapjack wanted me to find him. I asked him what he meant. Did he not know where Flapjack was?

"No one can see him but me," he said. "But he wants you to find him."

About a week later, my doorbell rang. On my doorstep was an army captain.

"May I come in?"

"Sure," I said. "But do I know you?"

"I'm afraid not. I was in your husband, Bryan's, company. I just got home recently."

That's when I recognized him. He was on the news just two days before. He'd been missing in action and had been found and brought home to great fanfare. It was a wonderful human interest story. The pangs of grief hit me though, for my husband and all the husbands who wouldn't be coming home at all.

"I wanted to come and find you," he said, "because, well, before I went missing, well, let me tell you a story. Our Hummer was attacked at a checkpoint. The enemy ambushed us. They hit us with a grenade and some of the shrapnel entered my leg and the leg of my buddy, John. The best John and I could do was to crouch on the floor of the vehicle and hope that our backup would take care of the enemy. Well, unbeknownst to us, the enemy was advancing quickly. Bryan was safe behind a dune. When he saw John and me in our predicament, he found an opportunity to pick off two soldiers who were about to get us. Then he rushed out and dragged me from the vehicle. Then he ran back again and got John. He shielded John from fire with his own body, getting hit in the process. They got Bryan bad, I'm sorry to say, and he died right after dropping John and me behind the dune. The enemy advanced on us as we made our escape. I managed to get away, but John wasn't so lucky. Did your husband ever tell you about us?"

"No," I said, flabbergasted with pride for my husband's actions. "But don't take offense. He never really said much about his army buddies. I think he preferred to keep them to himself."

"Well, we got pretty close towards the end there. Bryan gave us nicknames. He called me Twinkle Toes, because I was a pretty good runner. And because John loved pancakes—downed at least five of them any time they were available—Bryan called him Flapjack."

I wasn't sure what I'd just heard. "I'm sorry," I said. "Did you just say he called John *Flapjack*?"

"Yes, ma'am."

You remember how I started this off by saying I'm not much of a believer in anything? My unbelief was about to get another jolt.

After the captain left, I picked up Matthew from school.

I stared at him in the rear-view mirror. "Honey, you know how you always say that Flapjack wants me to find him?"

"Yeah."

"Does he say where he is?"

"He told me just a little while ago."

"And where did he say he was?"

He looked out the window at the swirls of trees rushing past it. "He said he's underneath the sand."

With the help of the captain and some kind souls at military headquarters, we were able to pinpoint the prison camp to where John, a.k.a. Flapjack, would have been taken. By that point, American forces had overrun the enemy and captured the territory. What's more, they'd uncovered a mass grave of bodies, former prisoners who died under torture, their bodies haphazardly plowed over with heaps of desert sand. The autopsy revealed that John had probably died at night. They told me the exact date they believed he died. I remembered it: it was a particularly warm night in early June. The night of Flapjack's first conversation with my son.

I'm proud to say that, through a pretty tenacious campaign of phone calls to cut through a mile of red tape, I was able to help recover John's body so that he could be shipped home for a proper burial.

The doctor was right, in a way: Flapjack did go away. It was the day after the funeral that Matthew stopped talking to Flapjack altogether.

I finally got up the nerve to ask him about it one night while tucking him in.

"You haven't been talking to your friend Flapjack at all, have you?"

"No," he said, with more than a touch of sadness in his voice.

"Why not?" I asked.

"Because he's gone. He told me he can't talk anymore. I'm sad about that. But he wanted me to tell you that he says thank you."

"So that's it?" I asked. "He's gone?"

"Yeah, he went back into the picture."

He pointed at the framed newspaper clipping beside his bed. I went over and looked at the caption and found John's name.

I know there's a lot of sadness in the story, but there's something about it gives me great peace when I'm alone. Maybe if Flapjack still existed somewhere, somehow after he died, then my husband did too.

Click, Click, Click

I believe we all pay the price for our sins. Sooner or later, we all pay.

Five and a half years ago, I got the promotion to senior sales rep and the guys and gals in the office threw a little after-hours party at the local tavern. Well, there was this intern, Judy. Judy and I got a little too close that night. We'd been getting a little too close all season long. That night we discovered we'd fallen for each other like pebbles in an avalanche.

Now, one of the perks of the promotion was that I got to assemble a team to represent the Western division. I'll give you ten guesses who the first person was that I picked for the team. It worked out fine. Judy and I would be traveling together. All under the auspices of business. I guess I had what every man would possibly want.

Trouble was I also had a wife.

The sad thing is that Arlene and I had started off great. We were young and professional, fresh out of college, ready to take on the world.

Maybe we got married too soon. Maybe it's just that I hadn't yet tasted life. I don't know.

Maybe I just make too many excuses.

I don't want to talk about the day we found out Arlene had that lump. Or the day we found out that it had metastasized and spread to her lymph nodes. Stage four.

I was as good a husband I could be during that dark time. I cooled it off with Judy. Yeah, I had to deal with the cold shoulder, the vindictive rants on my voice mail, the threats to tell Arlene. I didn't care, I told her.

Four months later, Arlene passed.

And I was suddenly free. That's the hardest thing to admit.

It was chilly between Judy and I at first. But you know some women. They give in eventually. You just have to know the empty place they have, and they all have it. It's in there somewhere just waiting for a guy like yours truly to come along and set up shop.

And so we were back together, only with one truly significant change: I was now a committed bachelor. I wasn't about to be tied down ever again.

Judy was surprisingly OK with that arrangement.

The next five years went by in a flash. I saw other women, Judy saw other men, and we saw each other frequently. It was a great arrangement. Then she started whining to me about the old biological clock and all that. And what could I say? I gave in. *Fine, we can take it a bit more seriously,* I told myself. *I am getting older. I should settle down.* I'd spent years depriving myself of the life I wanted due to my marriage to Arlene, and I was ready to move on.

Arlene.

I hadn't even realized the anniversary was here. It was something in the air I think that did it. A waft of patchouli coming off the mail girl as she passed by my office, maybe. But *something* triggered the memory of Arlene. I felt a darkness come over me. I looked at the calendar. It was five years to the day that she died.

The phone on my desk rang. I silently cursed my receptionist for going to lunch so early and leaving the phones on night service so that the calls would be assigned randomly to the sales team. And I cursed myself for not shutting my own phone down. I had a lot of work to do to prepare for my upcoming business trip to the West Coast.

I picked it up.

A tiny bit of static, and then *click, click, click, click …*

It was steady, like the ticking of the proverbial time bomb. I didn't have time for this. After two hellos with no response I hung up.

I realized I was still shaken by the sudden recollection of Arlene and the time she was sick and wasting away before my eyes. Poor thing went to her grave never knowing that I'd cheated on her. Was I remorseful? Sure. But I think I'd more than made up for it by being at her side for the duration of her illness.

My ride home was tedious as ever. As I sat in the million-wheeled worm of rush hour, inching along, I suddenly found myself thinking about the noise I'd heard on the phone. It ticked me off that our IT department couldn't get their networks to function properly. Poor communications systems could cost us all sales, period. I made a mental note to send them an email when I got home.

But by the time I got home, I had no fight left in me and decided I would just kick back with a little bourbon and baseball.

When I turned the TV on, there it was: *click, click, click, click.* The same sound as before. It was clearer now, and I could tell it wasn't an electronic sound; it was a *metallic* one. Like the sound of a gear and sprocket. And I could tell now that there was a decided rhythm to it. It seemed to start off slow, then speed up slightly and grow a little in volume. It went that way for about twenty seconds and then the whole sequence started over.

Maybe my cell phone was interfering somehow. I turned it completely off. Nothing changed. I turned the TV off and on again, but the clicking sound was still there. Standing there, remembering Arlene, and suddenly recalling the steady rhythm of the beeping machines in hospice, I was seized with a hitch in my breath. It was the kind you get in the middle of the night when you get up to use the bathroom. You know what I mean? When you shut the door and lock it, even though no one is around? You do that because it's the time of night when your mind is still soft from dreams and all logic has gone out the window. And so while you're standing there you think you just might catch a peripheral glimpse of some figure poking its eyeless head around the doorway at you only to vanish again when you turn towards it.

I'm not saying I speak from experience here.

All I'm saying is that I found myself thinking of Arlene again. And that the clicking on the TV, and the phone, it all pressed on me like Chinese water torture.

Logic prevailed, and I resolved to get to the bottom of this thing. I hit "record" on the DVR and let it run for a few minutes. When I played it back, there was the clicking sound. *Good*, I thought. *It's there in physical form. I'm not hallucinating.*

My brother-in-law is a recording engineer and producer. He's got a professional studio built in his basement with all kinds of electronic gadgetry that would make Q from the *James Bond* films green with jealousy. So my next step was to make this bit of recording transportable. I was able to send it to an FTP server on my laptop and save it that way to a shared folder.

My laptop screen was hurting my eyes. My heart sank a little when I realized the reason why: the screen was flickering. Slowly at first, then speeding up, and then starting over after about twenty seconds.

I didn't bother to call my brother-in-law to tell him I was on my way.

Luckily it was after dinnertime, so he wasn't in the middle of a session when I showed up. He greeted me warmly; he must have sensed that I had something on my mind.

He accessed the shared folder on his network and brought up the file. By hooking up some doo-dad to a whoosy-whats and then routing the something to the main bus of the yadda yadda, he isolated the audio track of the baseball game.

He heard it too, thank God.

He was even able to lower all the noise associated with the game.

"This tells me something," he said. "The noise isn't coming from the program. It's on a completely different channel. It's as if someone got ahold of the game and then recorded his own clicking sound over it before broadcasting."

"So what are you saying?" I asked him queasily.

"I'm saying I never heard of something like that happening. These programs do go through a process before airtime, but they would catch any noises like this in post-production. This is Major League Baseball we're talking about here. They're not exactly some two-bit cable access show with no budget for audio engineering. Whatever this is, it's coming from your DVR."

"It's also coming from my phone at work," I said.

He paused, looking at me as if to assess whether or not I was joking. Then he shrugged his shoulders. "Maybe some interference in the area. Sunspots can do a lot of damage. Look up to see if there's been any sunspot activity lately."

It was awkward after that. I got the feeling he regarded me as a little loopy for telling him what I'd just told him. We chatted a bit off the subject and then said our goodbyes.

When I got home, the radio alarm clock was on in my bedroom. This was the room I'd shared with Arlene, and even once with Judy when Arlene was away for a weekend. The radio was blaring, and the *click, click, click, click* could be heard loud and clear.

Maybe I just needed to get away. Exhaustion, that's what it was. I'd been preparing for this West Coast trip for a while. The meetings would be over and I'd have some time to spend in the sun. That's what I needed. I probably mis-set the alarm clock.

I remembered then that I still had to confirm my flight online. I logged on. The screen flickered, this time going completely off and then on again to that miserable rhythm. So I called the airline. *Click, click, click,* louder than ever. I couldn't hear the prompts.

I wound up not being able to confirm the flight.

When I got to the airport the next morning, I met Judy there and told her that I wasn't able to confirm.

She looked at me with those sweet blue eyes of hers and said, "You might be able to do it in person."

Well, when I got to the customer service desk, they told me that they'd considered my lack of confirmation a cancellation, and that they'd have to book me on a later flight. OK, fine. I was too anxious and frustrated to argue it. I told sweet Judy to go on without me. I'd meet her a little later.

It wasn't till a few hours after I'd landed that it was confirmed: Judy's flight, the one I was supposed to have been on, had gone down over Ohio. There were no survivors.

* * *

Judy's funeral was a solemn affair on a beautiful sunny day in early September. I stood there on the ground, watching the coffin in disbelief.

Right after Judy's death—I mean that very night—the clicking stopped on my cell phone; after I got home, my work phone, my radio and TV, everything was silent. Now, the human mind is a natural maker of patterns, and naturally attributes certain effects to certain causes. So had it been Arlene causing the sounds the whole time?

The truth is, I don't know.

What I do know is the extent of my own pattern-making ability. I realized it when I stood watching the coffin being lowered into the grave and hearing the lowering mechanism with its steady, metallic *click, click, click*, speeding up slowly as gravity pulled my Judy into the ground.

Ghost Lake

"You can't fire me!"

"Grover, calm down," I said, sounding desperate even to my own ears. "Listen, I'm sorry, OK?"

"You're not sorry," Grover growled. "I expected better from you, Danny."

His words made me feel like a traitor. Who was I kidding? I felt that way before I even pulled up to my childhood vacation home that my parents had abruptly decided to sell after running into some cash flow problems. I suspected those cash flow problems had a lot to do with their lavish lifestyle. Apparently their habit of spending money recklessly without any thought for the future had caught up with them. Not that that was Grover's problem. He didn't deserve this.

He had been nothing but loyal to our family, even if his sour disposition made him difficult to deal with. He had always done his job. And I know he lived for this job. He had no children, no family, and no friends as far as I knew. And I'd known him all my life. He had always been kind to me and I suspected that's why my parents had sent me to fire him. They hadn't had the courage to do it themselves; after all, he had only tolerated them. Rightfully so.

Silently, I studied him trying to come up with the words to soften the blow I'd just dealt. He had a shovel in his hand and one foot planted on it. He leaned his lanky body against the shovel and looked towards the lake that bordered the back of our home. It hurt me to be my parent's messenger. Grover's presence had been the one constant during my tumultuous childhood. I could always rely on the recalcitrant, octogenarian groundskeeper to be there for me, especially after Camden's death.

I mentally shook away that memory. I waited for Grover to speak. His lips were drawn in a tight line and his pointy chin seemed thinner with age. I watched him as he chewed carefully before spitting out a glob of dark chewing tobacco not even an inch away from my foot. I scooted my foot back and Grover laughed darkly.

"Get out of here, kid. We don't have anything else to say to each other."

"My parents will gladly pay you for your services, Grover, up until the end of the month," I responded weakly.

Grover kept walking, not even acknowledging my words. I followed behind him as he rounded the corner leading to the back of the house. Something snagged my ankle and I went stumbling to the ground. As I dusted myself off, I looked around, not seeing anything that could have made me fall, cursing my own clumsiness. I then looked around again, but there was no sign of Grover.

I placed my hands on my hips and looked left and right. I didn't know where he could have possibly disappeared to so quickly. Off in the distance, I saw a bird swooping low in the sky. It landed somewhere in the trees that made up the forest that bordered my childhood home. The same home where we had lost my older brother so many years ago. It felt like yesterday and if I closed my eyes and allowed my brain to roam, I relived the nightmare of that day. I heard her screaming, my mother, as she struggled to pull my brother's body out of the water and to shore.

His body had been lifeless, of course. The medical examiner would eventually inform us that he had been dead for days. His skin, which had once been an olive color, had turned gray. His features, once handsome, had been puffy when mother found him, almost deformed by the elements and the fish that had fed off of him. She had found him on a day like this one when the sun was going down. Her screams of sorrow tore from her body and I had shuddered at the sound.

I felt a hand touch my shoulder, startling me back to the present, and I turned quickly around. Grover stood there, expressionless, all anger from earlier gone.

"What are you still doing here, boy? Didn't I tell you to leave?"

"Grover—"

"It's almost dark, kid. Get gone. I'm not responsible for you no more." He turned to walk away again and I didn't bother to follow him this time.

What did he mean, "Not responsible for me no more?" I didn't think much of it and instead headed back to my car. I carefully made my way across the driveway, trying to avoid spraining my ankle in the mud. I'd never been the athletic type, more prone to falling over my own feet than I was to scoring a touchdown.

Grover was right; it was getting dark and my poor eyesight was even worse in the dark. I swore years ago that I would man up and get LASIK surgery, but I still hadn't done so. As I turned to open my car door, I thought I saw something in my peripheral vision. I looked towards the woods, but there was nothing there. I reached for the door again and this time, reflected in the glass was a figure who stood within touching distance behind me. Thinking it was Grover I turned around, only to find no one standing there.

I gulped. My eyes weren't *that* bad. I convinced myself it was just Grover brooding, but doubt filled my mind. There was no way Grover could have possibly moved that fast. Something felt off and as I opened my door, I tried to shake that feeling. I started my car and began to back up slowly. I heard a thud, followed by a bark that turned into a yelp. I slammed on my breaks. I could hear whimpering coming from behind my car. I quickly climbed out. Upstate New York wasn't exactly the mecca for stray dogs. What was a dog doing on our property?

I recognized the dog that lay behind my car almost immediately. White and scruffy with brown paws—I couldn't believe my eyes. My parents had said he had went missing years ago—years before I had gone to college, when I had first been sent off to boarding school.

With shaking hands, I reached for him. "Scruff?" I said as I reached out to his prone figure. He groaned and looked at me. Something about his eyes were different and as I reached out to touch him, he growled at me, stilling my hands from their course.

"It's OK, Scruff. It's me. Danny." I reached for him again and he lunged at me. I fell backwards and he limped away into the woods that led to the lake.

I scampered behind him, trying to keep up. The path through the woods was barely illuminated now. I could hear him moving through the woods, but the sun was going down and it was becoming even more difficult to see him.

"Scruffy!" I called. "Come back, boy."

I saw a flash of white between the trees and followed, going deeper into the woods. I noticed that the woods grew thicker then and I tried my best to avoid the low-hanging branches that suddenly seemed to cast ominous shadows across the ground. There were no signs of Scruffy anymore, but in the far off distance I swear I heard whimpering. I thought I heard a sound behind me and turned towards it. Nothing was there, but I couldn't shake the feeling that something was wrong. I felt as if I was being watched and that feeling kicked my imagination into overdrive. My heartbeat began to race and I picked up the pace, knowing that the woods led directly to the lake and from there I could find my way back to the car.

I felt panicked as I made my way quickly through the woods. I didn't know if it was just my imagination because I was already afraid, but the sun seemed to be going down faster than I expected. When I hazarded a look behind me, there was nothing there but darkness. I ran then, pushing against the limbs that got in my way, scratching my face against leaves that cut into my skin. My glasses were knocked askew and I was panting from exertion when I finally found myself stumbling out of the forest.

And it was then that I froze. I heard—no. That wasn't right. But I swear I heard my brother calling out to me.

"Danny."

Clear as day, I could hear him and my first inclination was to run. But then I saw Scruffy seated at the edge of the dock, sitting there looking at the water, whimpering. I approached the dog, who stared transfixed at a spot in the lake. I moved towards him, although every part of my brain screamed for me to run. It was almost as if I had no control over my movements anymore. My body moved on its own accord towards the dock and I could hear my brother calling for me now with a sense of urgency. I could hear the splashing and then Scruffy began to bark and snarl, still staring into the lake.

I was running then, no longer propelled by the invisible force, but propelled by my desire to save my brother. I ran to the dock and saw him there, partially submerged, trying his best to stay afloat, thrashing and fighting an invisible foe.

"Camden!" I screamed as I reached out my hand to him. I couldn't swim. I was afraid of the water. Always had been, even before Camden died.

Camden died. My mind repeated that statement over and over. What was going on? This couldn't be Camden. He was already dead. I realized then that Scruffy was gone and within seconds I was in the water. I didn't know how I had gotten there. One moment I was reaching forward and the next I was inside the lake fighting for my life. I panicked as I began to sink into the depths of the lake. I held my breath and my chest began to burn as I flailed around trying to get back to the surface. Something floated past me and I screamed just before water began to fill my lungs.

I knew then that I was going to die. I was going to join my brother.

But then I felt hands pulling me towards the surface. Strong hands that gripped me under my underarms and dragged me back up to the dock.

I coughed and sputtered. I sat up on all fours and began to shudder, taking in large gasps of breath. My lungs still burned, my whole body for some reason ached, and finally when I could breathe again without wheezing I realized there was someone standing in front of me. I shook as I looked up slowly, expecting the worst.

Grover stood there looking at me with concern. "Give me your hand, Danny."

I did as I was told and he helped me stand up. He looked at the lake, which was still now. The sun was almost down, turning the sky a dark orange with hints of purple on the horizon.

"Thank you. For saving me," I managed to squeak out, adjusting my glasses.

Grover gruffly nodded, never taking his eyes off the water.

Finally, he looked at me and said, "Get gone, kid."

I didn't need any convincing; I turned and headed towards my car, which still stood in the driveway with the driver's door open.

"Hey, kid!" Grover called, stopping me in my tracks.

I turned around.

"Don't come back here." He then turned away from me and walked to the edge of the dock, staring into the water with a sad look on his face.

I didn't respond. I just hustled to my car and drove away. When I hazarded a look back less than a minute later, I thought I saw a figure watching me from the porch. I assumed it was Grover, but didn't get a chance to think much of it when my phone suddenly rang.

"What's up, Mom?" I said immediately knowing it was her.

"Is it done?" she asked. Her voice sounded odd.

"You mean, did I do your dirty work? Then yes. I let Grover go."

"Don't get snarky with me, Danny," her voice caught and I immediately felt bad.

"I'm sorry—it's just been … quite a day," I said with a sigh.

"For me too…." She let her voice trail off and I knew something was wrong. She was normally carefree and not nearly so sensitive.

"What's wrong, Mom?"

"You know what today is, don't you?"

"Ummm … the twenty-fifth." I was clueless as to why she was so concerned about the date.

"Ten years," she said softly. "Ten years today since I found Camden dead."

Bloody Church Bells

The church bells echoed through the air and the taste of silver pennies lingered on my tongue as my head dangled from side to side. My hands felt numb as the tight ropes bit into them, keeping me strung up on the cross against my will. I looked ahead of me and watched the three of them hold hands and stare down at what looked like a Bible. I could see it now, the craziness that enveloped them. Never in my wildest imagination did I think that Melissa, Janet, and Tracy would be absolute maniacs who probably should have been on some serious antipsychotics. Fear drilled a hole into my chest as my heart pounded so hard that I could hear it in my head. It was truly that loud. On top of that, my head felt woozy from being knocked over with a steel ornament that lay on the floor near the entrance of the church. My chest started to close up and the fear of being killed kicked in.

I suffer from anxiety and this pushed me over the edge. I gasped for air and frantically pulled and tugged at the ropes in hopes of being freed. A part of me knew that I should draw as little attention to myself as possible but I couldn't help myself. I felt powerless and all I wanted was to jump out of my own body and escape this place. The church was once a place I regarded as safe. If anything, after growing up on the wrong side of the suburbs, the church was the one place that struck me as salvation. There's no room for woes and violence in a holy place and yet here I was, strung up to a cross by three crazy women who had knocked me over the head. I could have suffered a hemorrhage and died!

All of a sudden the three women began to scream and wail at the top of their lungs before launching a barrage of kicks onto the Bible in perfect synchrony. *How bloody blasphemous! I* thought. Above all my fear and anxiety, the anger and frustration of watching my Holy Book being so blatantly disrespected in a place I called home made my blood boil. *How dare they do this? They spent a year in this place, training to become nuns and learning all about our religion, and yet here they stand, abusing a real believer and disrespecting the Holy Book.* I couldn't control myself. All I could see was red and before I knew it, the most unexpected yet obvious words escaped my dry and cold lips. "You will burn in hell for this!"

They suddenly stopped. All three of them stopped kicking the Bible and just stood deadly still. It dawned on me that I had stripped their attention away from the book and drew it right back to me. I guess, as a nun, standing up for something as sacred as the Holy Book made me feel a sense of optimism and pride but that was quickly erased when I realized that they had all turned to face me, biting on their lower lip and staring blankly.

Was it worth it? Inside I was screaming and pleading to God for help and on the outside I tried to remain calm but the tears that rolled down my face told a different story. The women began to walk. In perfect rhythm they took strides towards me, almost like robots who were programmed to act the same. Not once did they take their eyes off me, nor did they blink. As they got closer to me the three of them began to pull off their clothes until all they had on was underwear. I panted and swallowed chunks of air in hopes of controlling my anxiety, but it didn't help.

All three women were about the same size and had the same brunette hair, black eyes, and pale skin. They made their way to the main altar not more than three feet away from me. I felt as if my time was coming to an end and I'd be seeing God soon. Without a shadow of a doubt, they were going to kill me and I had no idea why. They were stand-up women. I may not have known them well, but I knew them well enough to know that this wasn't normal.

Poised and respectful. That's what they struck me as. And yet, here they were, about to commit a heinous crime. I was so fixated on my own fearful thoughts that I didn't realize what was happening right in front of me. I could see yellow liquid soaking through their underwear and then flowing down their legs. They were peeing in the church. It was disgusting and the fact that this pure place was being tarnished by impure urine made me want to throw up. They were torturing me without even touching me. Never in my life had I been so angered.

I wanted to kill them.

Just when I thought it couldn't get any worse, the three women smiled as their urine created a small puddle on the ground. They bent down and dropped their palms into the puddles, soaking up the urine as much as they could. *What are they doing?* I wondered.

They straightened their petite spines and stormed towards me. I pulled my head back against the cross, trying to shake loose from the ropes tying my hands and legs to the cross, but it was futile. The vile women shoved their hands on my face, wetting my skin with their filthy urine. I wailed and screamed in anger and absolute disgust.

I was just a twenty-eight-year-old nun who had tried to build a life around my belief in the Lord. I gave up my worldly desires and abandoned a chance to study law at the University of

Cambridge because I felt like the church was my true home, my salvation, the one place I could be myself without wearing a fake face. I believed I could find a family in this place and I had.

Every person in this church who had devoted themselves towards our common cause made me feel part of something greater. For the first time, I had felt like my life had a meaning, had a purpose, and in just one afternoon these horrendous women stole ten years of my life from me. They tarnished the one place that I loved in this entire world. I wanted them to just drop dead and die. Just as things seemed to become futile the church doors began to rattle. A voice seeped through the mahogany wood doors. It was Father Matthew! He kept banging on the doors, screaming for someone to open them immediately. Later I learned that Gregory, the courtyard cleaner, was about to leave for the night when he saw me being followed by the three crazy women. He thought nothing of it until he saw one of them had knocked me over the head. He wasn't sure what had transpired so he proceeded to find Father Matthew and have him deal with the matter.

The women ran towards the third row from the front, dropped down to their knees, and looked as if they were searching for something. Suddenly, the church doors flew open and Father Matthew rushed inside, staring at me in utter disbelief.

"What's going on?" he asked. As he sprinted down the aisle, I watched as the women sprang up and ran towards him, driving knives straight into the side of his body. All three of them pierced his skin and twisted the knives into his torso. He began to fall; blood sprayed out of his body as they pulled the knives out. I tried to scream but the shock from what had just transpired locked my jaw in place. Hairs all around my body stood on end and goosebumps crawled up my skin. My throat clammed up and my eyes created even more tears. They killed Father Matthew and I was next.

"Why are you doing this?" I managed to ask.

They ignored me. Instead, they dropped down and got on all fours. Lowering their head, they stuck out their tongues, licked up Father Matthews' blood, and used their hands to cover their faces in his blood. They were completely mental. Laughter finally escaped their bloodied lips and they got up and bolted towards me. Finally, a scream exited my throat but it was short-lived. They drove the blade across my face, slicing my cheek open. Blood oozed from my face and I cried out in pain but all it did was further enhance the pain coursing through my body. I could literally feel air penetrating the cut and seeping into my mouth. The women began to howl and then it happened.

They looked to me with huge, menacing smiles on their faces as their eyes rolled to the back of their skulls and they spoke with a deep, manly, distorted voice.

"Long live Lucifer, King of Hell! Our one true savior!"

Within a second, all three women ran the blades across their throats. Blood gushed out of their necks as they fell to their knees, laughing and gurgling. I was rescued an hour later by the police and paramedics.

Those girls weren't crazy after all. They were possessed! Since that day I've realized, without a shadow of a doubt, the devil is real ... and it's my job to help as many people as possible.

High Desert Freeze

gazed down the red rock desert trail and then over at Star huffing along next to me. Her legs were still pumping pretty hard but her head was dropping a bit and I wondered if she needed a break. We'd been hiking for two hours straight and there'd been a lot of steep inclines we'd hit along the way.

"You doing OK?" I asked.

"Yeah, I'm fine," she said. "Just got a little cramp in my thigh. Let me rub it out for a second."

She stopped walking and started pressing her hands into her upper leg. I lifted my water bottle and took a drink. It was dry out here. Really dry. I'd been to the high desert in Utah before but had never hiked it and the air was like something from Mars.

Star stood back up. "Check that out," she said, pointing a little off to the right from where we were.

The early evening sunlight gave the horizon a wavy orange look and at first I couldn't see anything but then I saw what she was talking about. There was some kind of writing on a rock the size of a small elephant just to the right of the trail.

"Wow. Had you heard anything about something like that?" I asked.

"Nope. Nothing."

We were out deep in desolate nothingness and there'd been barely any guide markings so far so it was odd to see something like this.

"Want to check it out?" I asked.

Star bit down on her lip and looked around. "I don't know, A.J. It's not that long before the sun starts to set. We really should start heading back now."

I rubbed my chin and looked west. The sun was in that sort of in-between state. Not quite setting, but getting there. We had maybe forty-five minutes of real light left before things got a little shadowy.

"Well, we've got our headlamps for the way back," I said. "And we probably shouldn't need them until close to the end anyways."

Star pushed her blonde hair back from her aviator glasses and gave a little nod. "OK, let's check it out."

Good girl.

We started moving again and as the trail veered right I could see that there was in fact a semi-hidden side trail where the rock with the writing was. After about five minutes we got to the side trail and the big rock and both of us stopped cold.

This is the trail of Frozen Eyes.
His burial ground lies a mile deep from here. Every night as the sun sets his ghost rises to roam the trail. If you lock eyes with him your heart will freeze.
Do not be on this trail at sunset.

"Ha, that is awesome," I said.

Star didn't say anything and looked back down the trail from where we came.

"Oh, come on, Star," I said.

She didn't say anything and looked back at the writing.

I stepped onto the side trail and traced my hand along the white paint.

"A.J., don't," Star said.

"*Star*, it was just somebody screwing around that wrote it."

She didn't say anything but I knew she could fall for stuff like this. Her parents had named her Star, after all. It wasn't exactly a family of hard-science types.

"Yeah, maybe. But we've only got so much sunlight left and it's going to take us a good two hours to get back to the Jeep."

"Well, let's just go down the trail real quick and see if there's really a burial ground. And then we can turn back quick and get going, OK?"

Star went quiet for a couple of seconds. "OK," she said and stepped onto the side trail next to me.

We started hiking again and after about a hundred yards the trail curved a bit left between two ten-foot high walls of rock that stretched for about fifty or sixty yards and then straightened out again. We then hit a slight incline of ten or so feet and then the trail wiggled around some sharp rocks. I noticed another trail splinter off to the left about ten yards ahead that really blended into the terrain from this direction. I took a quick glance back. The rocks we'd just navigated through did a nice job of hiding the part of the trail we'd just hiked over.

I turned my eyes forward again and smiled. Nothing but smooth, straight trail for the next quarter mile.

The sun had dipped a bit, giving the rocks a fiery look, and I watched a jackrabbit dart out from behind a rock just north of the trail to a single green shrub that was the first plant life we'd seen in over an hour. Star was walking briskly next to me like she couldn't wait to get this over with and I suddenly felt a bit bad about pushing her to come down here.

But hey, it'd be good for her to conquer her silly supernatural fear.

We hiked for another few minutes and a scattering of white tombstones seemed to almost magically appear in the dark blue horizon at the end of the trail. Star saw them too and she stopped hiking. I stopped and looked at her.

"Star," I said.

She stared hard at the little cemetery ahead. I'd never bought into any of her cosmic/spiritual nonsense, but it *was* a little eerie how she could sense things sometimes. She'd often pick up her phone just before it rang, was amazing at predicting storms—even when the sky and the weather report said "sunny and blue skies"—and despite knowing absolutely nothing about football, had told me a bunch of times to bet big on huge NFL underdogs that ended up kicking ass.

But intuition was one thing.

No way I was buying into the ghost of Mr. Frozen Eyes.

Star nodded and we started walking again. The tombstones got larger and I counted seven of them. A minute later we were standing at the cemetery's edge.

The desert sprawled out beyond the burial ground in a panoramic stone sea of red, almost like a cemetery at the edge of the world. Even Star's face had lit up at the sight of it.

"Not too bad, huh?" I asked.

"Yeah, this is amazing."

We stood there for a minute and then Star tapped me on the shoulder. "We really do need to get going now, A.J. I'm serious; we don't want to be wandering around out here too late."

"OK," I said and snapped a picture with my phone. "Just let me check out these tombstones real quick. I want to see if one of them actually says 'Frozen Eyes.'"

"A.J., no," Star said sharply. "Don't walk in there."

I took a deep breath and let it out. Hell, she'd come this far for me and I didn't want to push my luck. "OK, babe," I said. "Let's get out of here."

We turned around and my skin felt a chill at the sight of the sun lowering before my eyes. "Yeah," I said again, "let's go."

As we walked back down the trail the sun dipped even more and shadows started to spread across the desert floor.

"Did the message say that Frozen Eyes comes out *at* sunset or *after* the sun sets?" Star asked.

Great, here we go.

"I honestly can't remember, Star," I said as we walked up a slight incline that I didn't remember being there before.

Star picked up the pace and after about five minutes the trail veered hard right around a trio of six-foot-tall arrowhead-shaped rocks. "Wait a second," I said and stopped. Star turned around and looked at me with a tight mouth and wide blue eyes. "I don't remember these rocks and I know we didn't make any big turns when we came out here." I looked behind me. "I think we screwed up."

"Ugh. *A.J.*," Star said.

"I know, I know," I said. "Come on, I think we're on a hidden side trail I noticed when we were going to the burial ground, but it blends into the main trail when you're going the other way. We walked onto it without realizing it. We just need to get back on the first trail and we'll be out of here."

As we started heading back, a heavy shriek pierced the sky like a sonic wolf howl and my heart felt like it'd been stabbed with a knife. I looked at Star. The muscles in her arms and legs were shivering.

"Had to have been some kind of weird bird," I said as I looked over the sky and saw nothing.

"Yeah," Star replied without a trace of confidence.

The shriek rang out again and I grabbed Star's arm. "Come on, let's hustle," I said.

We jogged for a couple of minutes and then the straight trail popped into view. We hurried up to it and then went back to a brisk hike.

"Fun, huh?" I asked.

Star didn't say anything and looked back, peering hard into the distance.

"Do you see something?" I asked.

"I don't know," she said. "It's like I can see the light shifting against the trail."

"What does that mean?" I asked as I realized a big, white, full moon was now hovering just to the south of us.

"Like a bright white blast of light just flashed against the rocks then disappeared."

"I bet it was just the moon," I said.

"Yeah," Star said flatly.

We made it through the straightaway and then were back in the part with the smooth, curvy rock walls. It felt claustrophobic in here this time, like the walls were pressed tight against us like a second skin.

But they weren't.

We had a good three or four feet of space on each side and there was only another twenty or so feet to go.

"Run, A.J.!" Star shouted.

I started to look back but she just pushed me ahead.

"What is it?" I asked.

"Something ... something is behind us."

Star didn't finish and I didn't care. She was flipping out but I wasn't going to try and calm her down now. There'd be plenty of time for that when we got off this trail.

We made it out of the rock wall area and Star broke into a full sprint towards the trailhead about 200 yards away. I picked up speed and coasted up next to her. I chuckled at how ridiculous this was and then, with about twenty feet to go, a sharp pain spiked through my ankle as my foot twisted in a small rut in the ground. I fell to my knees and Star stopped running.

I looked back.

"No!" Star yelled.

A mass of swirling purple light as thick as our Jeep hovered about ten feet away. The light began to shape into a muscular chest and torso and then a rock-like neck and sharp-jawed, blurry face rose from the chest. A pair of hot-white glowing eyes appeared in the blur and my eyes locked on to them. I couldn't break his stare but I could see red streaks of light start to stretch across his cheeks like war paint as thick ropes of transparent white hair grew from his head and flowed over his shoulders.

And then my heart seized.

It was like a sheet of ice had wrapped itself around it; fist-clenching pain shot through my chest and into my neck and face. I thought I was having a heart attack as Frozen Eyes hovered towards me, letting out another war cry as my legs started to go numb.

"A.J., please, come on!" Star yelled. Her voice sounded far away and muddled as I felt myself sink deeper and deeper into the ghost's hard stare.

And then a pair of hands covered my eyes.

My chest suddenly warmed and I looked at Star.

The trance was broken.

I put my arm over Star's shoulders and pushed with my legs as hard as I could to stand up. Between me and Star we were able to get me to my feet and we staggered towards the trailhead and collapsed back onto the main trail.

A second later my heart started to feel better.

Star and I pushed ourselves up and I leaned against her to take the pressure off my ankle.

"It's going to be a long walk back," Star said.

"Just keep your eyes forward and we'll make it," I said.

The sky was now a dark purple and off in the distance a coyote howled. And as we made our way through the dry night, wind blowing across the high desert trail, I wondered just how much Star really knew about this world. About the things we usually couldn't see.

Because the days of me laughing at the idea of the spiritual world were over.

Frozen Eyes had taken care of that.

House Sitting

The rain poured down on the concrete steps as I ran up to the campus union. New jobs for the week were usually posted by now and I needed some quick cash to help cover this quarter's tuition. Pushing my way past a group of girls in red sorority sweaters, I made it to the top, pulled open one of the glass doors, and hurried inside.

A surge of hope ran through me when I saw that the big, cubed bulletin board that sat in the atrium was covered in flyers. I stomped some water off my feet and headed towards the job postings. As I walked past the lounge area with students studying and chatting, I wondered again how I'd let things get cut this close. Between the partial scholarship, my job, and the few hundred a month I got from my parents, it seemed like I should be making my payments easily—and yet here I was again, scraping for last-minute cash. My dad was always nagging me to set a hard budget every month and it looked like he was right.

When I got to the cube, I started to scan the jobs: baby sitter - $7/hr; calculus tutor - $10/hr; dog walker - $10/visit.

Bleh, bleh, and bleh. I needed real money fast.

And then my eyes got wide.

Needed: house sitter for this Saturday night. $200.

Bingo.

I punched the number into my phone and called it. After a few rings a man's voice answered.

"Hello," said a crisp, smooth voice.

"Yeah, hi. I'm calling about the house-sitting job you posted in the student union."

A few seconds of silence went by.

"Oh, the job posting! Excellent. I am so sorry my mind has just been swamped today."

"Oh, no problem," I said.

"Well, listen. Normally I would want to meet with you first but I'm going to be locked up with work tonight and all day tomorrow. How about this, could you be at the house at seven thirty tomorrow night and I can show you around and give you instructions then?"

My heart started to beat a little faster as it dawned on me that I'd be going to a complete stranger's home.

But two hundred dollars would take care of my immediate problems and I couldn't pass it up.

"Um, yeah. Sure. That sounds good."

"Excellent. I live at 817 Markson Street. Do you know where that is?"

"Um, yes, I know Markson. Just about a mile north of campus, right?"

"Yes, that is correct. And your name is?"

"My name is Anna."

"A pleasure to meet you, Anna. I'll see you tomorrow night at seven thirty."

The phone clicked off and I didn't even get his name.

I slid my phone back in my pocket and walked out of the union and went back to the dorm. The next day around 7:15 p.m. I drove over to Markson. The street was lined with older colonial homes and thick oak trees. I knew that a lot of money lived on the street and I'd heard a lot of the homes had been refurbished and were pretty modern inside. As I drove past a couple of kids riding bikes, I stretched my neck to read the house addresses.

"832, 827, 823," I read off.

"817."

It was a thick, white-bricked house with dark green shutters and a black Porsche in the driveway. The lawn looked like it hadn't been mowed in a few weeks but a nice little strip of yellow roses lined the front of the house up to the porch. I brought the car to a stop at the front of the house, shut it off, and got out.

A chilly breeze blew my hair around as I walked up the driveway to the porch. When I got to the single step I hopped up it and knocked on the heavy wooden door.

I rubbed my hands together and looked down the street at the two kids on their bikes. They stared at me and then one said something to the other one and they turned around and started to ride back the direction they came.

The click of the doorknob turning popped through the wood and the door opened. A thin man with short black hair parted neatly to the side stood in front of me. He smiled and held out his hand. "Anna?"

"Yes," I said as I shook his hand.

"Thank you so much for coming by. I'm Evan White. Please come in and we can go over things."

I stepped inside and he closed the door.

The house was neat and contemporary. A living room on my left had sort of a modernized 1950s style to it with a thin, silver table with short, beige wooden legs set in front of a lean, rust-colored leather couch. A fifty-or-so-inch flat panel hung on the white wall across from it and the floor was a beautifully cheery wood color. A smooth, beige wooden dining room table with a single white chair at each end filled up the room on my right. It was a big table for just two people and I wondered if that's where he ate with his wife every night—if he had one?

"Okay, Anna," Mr. White said as he walked into the living room, "this will be real simple for you and there are only two things that I need you to be very, *very* careful about. Number one, my wife, Sonja, is upstairs and has a bad case of the flu. She's had it now for a little over a week and is having a tough time kicking it so she needs to be completely undisturbed, so no going upstairs, OK?"

The upstairs part was no problem but I wasn't crazy about being sandbagged with a sick wife all of a sudden.

"No problem," I said.

"Okay, great," Mr. White said. "Number two, keep a very close eye on our cat. Don't let him wander upstairs. There're too many things for him to get into, and to be honest, my wife hates him."

OK ... wife hates the cat ...

"Yeah, sure. I love cats," I said.

"Great. He's a good cat. A little standoffish at first, but he's friendly once he gets used to you. Okay," Mr. White said as he clapped his hands together, "other than that, help yourself to anything in the fridge; we've got all the movie channels, and I should be back by ten tomorrow morning. Sound good?"

"Yeah, sounds great. Umm ... about—"

"Oh yes, your money. How about I give you a hundred now and the other hundred tomorrow?"

"Yeah, that would be great," I said.

"Excellent," Mr. White said as he took his wallet out of his back pocket. He opened it, counted out five crisp twenties, and handed them to me.

I put the money in my wallet and Mr. White suddenly hurried out of the room and ran up the stairs.

I was standing there, staring at the staircase, when a black cat with wide green eyes padded into the room. He stopped, stared at me for a second, and then jumped up on the couch and lay down.

Mr. White then came back down the stairs and into the living room. "Oh, great, you've met Buster. Okay then, I'm going to get going. Are you all set with everything?"

"Yeah, I think so," I said.

"Excellent. You two have fun together. And remember, neither of you go upstairs, OK?"

"Got it," I said.

"All right, very good."

Mr. White opened the front door and left.

I looked at Buster. "Just you and me, Mr. Buster."

Buster stared at me so intently I swore he was about to say something, but he just stretched out on the couch and closed his eyes.

I took the remote off the table, flipped on the TV, and sat down on the couch next to Buster. For the next two hours I sat there going back and forth between movies, concerts, and even watched something on the Military Channel about the "Airplane Graveyard" in Arizona. Mr. White hadn't been joking; he had just about every channel there was and it was definitely helping the time go by. I got up to see what was in the fridge and walked down the hall into a very nice kitchen with a sleek stainless steel fridge, oven, and microwave. The white tile floor shined like it had just been waxed and there was a lovely lemon scent in the air. It was odd that the lawn was sort of unkempt since everything else was so immaculate.

I opened the fridge to see it stocked with mostly fruit and vegetables. A couple of bars of goat cheese and fancy-looking beer bottles along with a half-dozen Diet Coke cans were lined up on the shelf of the door. I grabbed an apple, a bar of cheese, and a coke, and closed the door. I took a knife out of the drawer next to the sink and a small plate from the cabinet above it and went back into the living room.

And then I heard a scratching noise from upstairs.

Buster's head perked up and he looked at me with his big eyes. The scratching sounded like fingernails being scraped along the hallway. My heart tightened when I heard the turn of a doorknob.

I set everything down on the table and listened.

The fur on Buster's back had bristled into sharp points and he pressed himself against the far corner of the couch. I listened as the scratching got closer to the stairs, almost to the edge, and then it stopped. My hands had turned cold and clammy and Buster suddenly jumped off the couch and ran to the front door. He stared at me.

"Sorry, buddy. I can't let you out," I said. "Come back up here and let's watch some more TV."

Buster walked back over and curled into a ball with his eyes open and his ears pointed up.

I sat back down and switched to the Discovery Channel. Cracking open the Coke, I leaned back against the couch. A show was on about the solar system and as the computer-generated planets floated across the HD screen my eyes got heavy and I felt myself doze off.

My eyes popped back open when I heard high-pitched meowing coming from upstairs.

Damn it.

It took me a second to fully wake up and then I got up and went to the foot of the stairs.

Buster kept crying.

"Buster," I quietly called out. "Buster, come back down here."

Nothing.

I looked into the dimly lit hallway at the top of the stairs. Mr. White had told me not to go up there but Buster wouldn't come down.

I bit my lip for a couple of seconds and then began to climb the stairs.

Each step creaked under my foot and I hoped to hell the wife didn't hear me. As I reached the top I saw a narrow hallway with two rooms on each side. Three doors were closed with the one on the far left open. Buster cried again from the open room and I went towards it. I tiptoed past the other rooms and then peeked into the room where I heard Buster. The cat stood trembling in the center of the room with what had to be at least a hundred black-

and-white photos of a woman covering the walls and a single shelf on the far end.

I walked into the room and looked over the pictures. She was a pretty lady with amber-colored hair and big, almond eyes. It looked like in every photo she either had an ear-to-ear smile showing off slightly sharp, but otherwise perfect teeth, or her mouth was closed in a mischievous half smile. As I moved past the wall, I came to the shelf and saw a framed certificate laying on it.

It was a death certificate.

Sonja White's death certificate.

My hands trembled and I stepped back from the shelf.

The scratching started again and my skin chilled like I'd stepped into a meat locker.

Buster jumped into my arms.

I took a deep breath, let it out, and turned around.

The scratching had stopped and there was only one way out of here.

I walked to the doorway, bit down on my lip, and stepped back into the hall.

Emptiness.

The cat put its paws over my shoulders like a little kid holding on to his mom and I began to walk towards the stairs. A bone-rattling shriek from one of the rooms shook the walls and my heart just about smashed through my chest.

A door creaked open behind me.

I looked back. A woman with skin like wax paper wearing a wisp of a nightgown of wispy floated out of the far room on the right. Her cheeks were sunken and her wide-open mouth looked like an eight-ball without the white part. She raised her quivering thin arms and her black eyes narrowed into angry slits. I clutched Buster tight as she let out a scream that was like a lightning bolt crashing into my brain.

She started to come towards me.

I rushed down the stairs, flung open the door, and ran outside. Buster clutched at me as I stumbled over the thick grass to my car. When I got to it, I opened the door and the cat jumped onto the passenger seat. Jamming the key into the ignition, I hit the gas and floored it down the lit street. A few minutes later I was back on campus and as I drove towards my apartment, Buster walked onto my lap and lay down.

My hands quivered against the steering wheel and I didn't know if I should be pissed or simply relieved to have escaped Evan White's house of horror.

But I knew this: my nerves were shot and I probably wouldn't sleep for a month.

And as for the immaculate Mr. White, he could keep his hundred dollars.

Because I was keeping the cat.

Rita

fter two years of marital bliss, Margo and I had finally saved up for a two-story house in the suburbs. It was a beautiful old place. Exactly what we were looking for. Plus, they were selling it for a song. So we bought it, moved in, and enjoyed life as new homeowners. We even became fast friends with the young couple next door. Things were great.

For a short time, that is.

We slept in the master bedroom located at the top of a twelve-step staircase. One night I was awakened out of my sleep by a strange series of noises. In my sleepy fog I heard someone, or something, treading on the stairs. Light footsteps, almost like that of a cat, but heavy enough for the old wood to creak. Accompanying that sound was the sound of heavy breathing, as of someone laboring to climb the steps. As the breathing sound came closer, it suddenly stopped, and I heard a muffled thud just outside my door.

It jolted me fully awake and heard a soft sound like a child's coo. I nearly wet the bed.

I woke up Margo, the heaviest sleeper I've ever known, and asked her if she heard anything. Of course she didn't. When I told her about it the next morning, she dismissed it as the product of a tired mind.

Needless to say I was dog-tired that day. I went out and saw my friend Dave in his driveway.

"You look terrible," he said.

"Weird noises woke me up last night." I said, walking over to his property to meet him.

"Ah," he said. "So you finally met Rita."

"Rita?" I asked.

"Yeah," he said, smiling. "Nobody told you about Rita?"

"No."

"Huh," he said. "I mean, it doesn't make a difference. I remember a couple of the tenants that rented the room upstairs—what's now your master bedroom. They used to talk about Rita. I think she was an old tenant or something who died."

"They heard noises too?"

"Listen, you still have those old steam radiators in there?"

"I do."

"It was probably steam escaping. Steam can make some pretty strange sounds."

"But," I said, "I distinctly heard someone coming up the stairs, one by one, slowly, but faint, like something coming out of a speaker turned down very low. And then there was that sound like an object being dropped, and then that soft sound like a breathy voice."

Dave waved his hand at me. "House settling," he said. "The human ear will hear anything if it really wants to.""

Margo was working late that night. I had a chance to catch up on a backlog of invoices that had been piling up on me. Finally— it was around eight o'clock—I heard her puttering around in the kitchen. I called out to her.

I'll try to describe the sound that answered me. Have you ever stood in a fierce gale and tried to have a conversation with someone standing about twenty feet away from you? When their voice gets carried off and all you hear are tatters of it?

That's what I heard: a tattered sound. A thin sound full of intense sorrow. It came from all around me. It called out a name:

Jeffrey.

I don't think I need to remind you that my name is not Jeffrey.

Margo came home two hours later. By that point I'd had a few stiff drinks and turned on every light in the house.

She was skeptical about my story, as I knew she would be.

* * *

Through the real estate listing service, I managed to track down the previous owner.

Harry was a sweet-looking older gentleman who now resided in an assisted living facility. He could only talk for a little while, he said. Lunchtime was approaching. He sat in a wheelchair in the visitors' area.

I told him I was the one who bought the house he used to own.

His face went as gray as his hair.

I wasn't feeling too hot myself. "Are you OK?"

He looked me square in the eye, and in a shaky whisper, said, "Did she come back?"

Hot fear crept up into my neck. "Did who come back?"

"Rita," he whispered.

I only stared at him.

He nodded. "She came back, didn't she?"

The nurse came over at this point. "How are we?"

"Fine," Harry replied flatly, looking straight at me.

"Time for your medication," she said. Then looked at me. "He needs his lunch now."

She began to wheel him away, when he suddenly turned in his chair and grabbed me by the arm.

"You might think she's looking for *him*, but she's not."

"For whom?" I asked.

"*Jeffrey.*"

"Come on, Harry," said the nurse. "It's time for lunch."

When I got back home, Dave was hosing off the hood of his car. "Danged birds got me again. You'd think—hey, you alright?"

"What happened to Rita?" I asked.

"Oh, not that again. I don't even know if she existed. All I know's that it was just some story passed on from renter to renter." His face changed as if he'd just remembered something, and his expression became more serious. "Alright, there was the last guy. College kid. Nice guy. Very personable, actually. Seemed to have it all together. But he used to complain about something that would happen to him."

"Like what?"

"Like he'd get to the top of the stairs right before the door to the room, and suddenly he'd be overtaken by a profound sadness. Not like, you know, 'I'm having a bad day' or anything. This was an overwhelming anguish in the pit of his gut. It made him … ah, don't worry about it."

"You started this, Dave."

"Well, when the sadness came over him, he said he'd want to end it all. He'd just stand there at his door, trying to think of how he should off himself. He said he often thought about throwing himself down the stairs. You know, that's a pretty nasty drop—those hardwood stairs without any carpeting and all?"

I just stared.

"Listen," Dave said, "you're not telling me you're feeling anything like that, are you?"

"Not exactly," I said. "Then again, maybe I don't linger long enough for it to hit me."

"It's the power of suggestion," he said. "That's all anyone with a fertile imagination needs—an *idea*."

I went back into the house to touch base with Margo. She was sitting on our living room couch in tears.

I rushed over. "What's wrong?"

She shook her head. "I don't know. I went upstairs to clean the top of the banister. You know, there's that spot up there that needs a coat of varnish. I thought I'd dust it first. Then I just felt so depressed; I don't know what came over me. It was like everything in the world just receded from me like a tide."

Fear was welling up inside me. "You OK now?"

"Yeah," she said with a self-conscious chuckle. "I'll be fine. Maybe I'm just, you know, hormonal. I'm going to go back and finish dusting."

"No," I said forcefully. "Don't."

"What's the matter?"

"Nothing. Just please, don't do it."

"You're going to do it?"

"Sure. Later. I have to go out again."

"I see," she said with a smirk. "'Later' in manspeak translates to 'two or three days.'"

"I'm serious," I said. "Save it for me."

I left her then and went to pay Harry another visit.

* * *

I was ten minutes early for the after-lunch visitation hour. When I signed in, the nurse on duty told me that Harry had eaten very little that day and that he might not be in a very good mood when I saw him. He certainly was looking grim when I found him in the visitors' room.

I wasted no time. "Talk to me. Tell me about Rita."

He braced himself, taking a breath, then told me the story.

Rita was a young twenty-something prone to bouts of melancholia. She'd come off a string of bad relationships when she met this new guy, Jeffery. Right away, she was completely smitten. All smiles, all the time. He was her one, true love, she said.

Jeffery had a nice place that was near Main Street and all the village shops, so she started gradually moving stuff out of her apartment to go and live with him. At first it was little things like cookware and towels, things she could carry by the armload, but in time she'd gotten to the point where the only thing she had to bring was her clothes. So one afternoon she packed up a whole mess of them in a giant suitcase and brought it over to Jeffery's house. That morning she'd officially notified Harris and his wife, Lainie, that she was moving out in two weeks. When she got to Jeffrey's house, she found him with another woman. Of course, she was devastated. In a kind of heartbroken daze, she went back to her house—our house—lugged the suitcase up all twelve steps, dropped it at the top, then, after letting out a soft whimper, she swooned and went tumbling backwards down the stairs. She was dead by the time she hit the bottom.

"I've been hearing her last moments in that house," I said somberly.

His eyes were watery. And his voice from here on in was just a husk of what it had been up to this point. "It's women she hates. Women in love. All she wants is Jeffrey, but she's stuck, you see. She thinks all women are …" He put two fingers to his eyes. "She got my Lainie."

"Got her?"

He took a long, strengthening breath. "Lainie was heading out to the garden with a pair of shears when she tripped and fell face forward. The shears punctured her lung. It was ruled accidental due to a loose stone tile in the walkway that she tripped over. I knew the truth. She'd been complaining about that loose stone for weeks. She'd gotten into the habit of stepping over it. I saw her do it time and time again. We'd joke about it. I told her it was too much fun watching her step over it like that and that I wouldn't repair it because I was having so much fun."

Here the old man broke down at his sweet and painful reminiscence of the life he had shared with his beloved. I put a hand on his shoulder and he composed himself quickly.

"Those final days, she complained of a powerful sadness. I'm telling you, she killed herself. I rented the room out to single men after that, but each and every one of them complained about the same noises, and although they were too proud to mention the strange sorrow, I could tell a change had come over them. I sold the place and lived with my daughter for a short time before they put me in here. I have a weak heart, you know. And nightmares."

I left him there, telling him I'd visit more often and with happier news. By the time I got to the parking lot, I'd resolved to put the house back up on the market. I didn't care what was causing those noises. Maybe what I heard was steam, maybe the voice I heard was the wind. A friend of mine once heard a cat meow with a hairball in its throat and swore it sounded like a child saying hello. Maybe old Harry was nuts.

But I couldn't live in that house any longer. Call me naïve or a scaredy-cat. I just couldn't have the same cold skepticism as Dave.

When I got home, I called out for Margo.

"*I'm so glad you're back,*" she answered.

Nothing could have prepared me for the sight.

There was Margo, lying in a heap at the bottom of the stairs like a rag doll. Her head was caved in and blood pooled thickly around her. The rag and varnish lay a few feet away.

I put my hand to my mouth, and a small, horrible sound came out of my throat.

And then I heard the voice again.

"*You're back,*" it said. "*I'm so glad you're back.*"

The Heart of the Matter

ere's one for the books, as they say. It's a ghost story, for real. I only ask that you stick with me here for a moment while I give you the history.

I was twenty-three when my parents divorced after twenty-six years. Dad was forty-eight.

He remarried. A lovely woman by the name of Meg who had a Southern accent. She left him after only five years.

Dad lived on his own for a while, dating here and there. He finally settled down and remarried again at fifty-five. That one left after ten years, saying she "finally couldn't take it anymore."

Now, I had to hand it to him. No one could ever accuse Dad of not stepping back up to the plate. On his first visit to the social security office, he had to wait a long time. At the reception desk was a young woman. She had a yogurt she was eating and Dad said something about the strawberry pieces they put in there. Then he complimented her hair. She was thirty years his junior— young enough to be my younger sister. And if that wasn't awkward enough, she fell for him and they married. She stuck in there for only three years.

Dad was alone for a while after that. Then, when he was seventy-three, he met a lovely woman through an online dating service for older people. Dahlia moved in with him after only two weeks of dating. It also took only two weeks for her to move back out. She sent an email to me saying, "Good luck." Nothing else.

Around age eighty-two, Dad started showing all the usual signs of aging—slowing down, forgetting stuff, etc. As the only son, it was my duty to take care of him. I had the space anyway. And as a freelance web designer, I was home all the time. I also happen to be an amateur painter and had a spare room that I used as a studio, so I cleaned it up, took the old guy in, and set him up in it.

It was two weeks in when I finally realized why it was all those women couldn't take it anymore.

Dad was, to put it mildly, unbearable. Everything I did was wrong. He had always been a little fussy about things, like Felix Unger from *The Odd Couple*, but he must have gotten worse over the years.

"The stew vegetables are supposed to be in bite-sized chunks," he'd say, holding up a slice of carrot at the end of his fork. "Does that look like bite-sized to you?"

Then, "We're not in Florida here. Why is it so damned freezing?" Or, "We're not in Alaska here. Why is it so damned hot?"

Dad was the worst passenger you could ever have. "You drive like a blind cabbie!" he'd shout, waving his arms around frantically.

It got so that everything about him began to drive me nuts. Even the smell of his aftershave. It was this horrible mix of tobacco and too-sweet pine that made me sick to my stomach. It lingered in that room. He'd stand in front of the full-length mirror in my studio and slap it on his face each morning before inspecting his outfit from head to toe. I hated going in there. I hated the way he befouled my art studio.

I marveled at how some of those women stuck in so long. The only one I could really identify with was the one from the dating service who bailed out after two weeks.

It only took me a couple of days' worth of pondering to come up with a solution. Dad had enough interest from his real estate investments to leave a nice little nest egg for his only son.

And therein lies the beginning of the story. And the end.

Dad was diagnosed with a heart condition. The doctor said it had been "nothing short of miraculous" that Dad had survived without medication all this time. He prescribed a heart medication and charged me with the task of monitoring his dosage. One thing was certain: Dad could die without it.

Did you know that there's a certain heart medication on the market that bears a striking resemblance to a popular type of breath mint?

All it took was for me to scrape off the etched logo on the candy and then give it a quick dip into a solution of cornstarch and water. Once it was coated, you couldn't taste the mint.

No one can judge me for what I did. Any of those women will bear me out. I just couldn't take it anymore. Besides, that money would really take care of me for a while. I couldn't seem to hold on to a steady relationship. With that money—and Dad out of the way—I could start with a zero balance. I could finally live according to my dreams, as they say. I could develop my artistic skills.

I got myself a cat that I named Martha. A gorgeous calico. I named her after a Beatles' song.

So I guess you can say it all started with the cat. And this is how.

Dad had been gone for three weeks. I was in my newly reclaimed studio, painting a nice, serene landscape. The bequest money had not come in yet; it would be tied up in legal red tape for a while. Never to mind. I was already feeling the bliss of not having to deal with the old man anymore, the bliss of having my life back.

Martha padded by the studio, looked in at me, arched her back as her fur raised like a hedgehog's quills, and hissed at me.

Now I don't care who you are, when a cat does that, you stiffen. Especially a cat as sweet as Martha. I walked out to her but she scampered away, her little tail between her legs. I followed her into my bedroom, where she scampered underneath my bed.

Any cat owner will attest to how flighty those little guys can be at times. I figured it was nothing.

Until I went back into my studio. And that's when I smelled it: tobacco and too-sweet pine.

There was no mistaking it. It was definitely in that room. It wasn't overpowering. It's hard to describe it. Have you ever felt like you were being watched? Is it strange to think that you can be watched by an *aroma*?

It had lingered in that room since Dad's passing, of course. That was the logical solution. But if that was the case, then why was there that growing fear in the pit of my stomach?

The smell was suddenly gone. It didn't dissipate; it simply wasn't there anymore. Like the way water isn't there anymore when you shut the tap.

It was a strange feeling, but I didn't give it much thought. And I didn't feel guilty. I don't care what anyone says—Dad was living a miserable life and I helped put an end to that misery.

But it got so that when I went into that room, I began feeling a kind of despair that I'd never really felt before. It was this awful feeling—like sinking. I'd go in, work on whatever was sitting on the canvas, but then after a few strokes I'd have to drop the brush and leave the room.

Forget Martha. She wouldn't come near that room. I started to avoid it too.

But what can I say? I have an artistic drive, I guess. I couldn't stay away for long. Upon my first day back in the studio after a week, I felt that same sinking sensation. Let me try to describe it. It was the loss of an ice cream cone when you're five years old. That's exactly what it was. It was the entire world crashing down around you. Loss. Despair. The end of all happiness as you know it.

It wrenched at me. I started to hyperventilate. Then the smell came again and I left the room and threw up.

My doctor said it was anxiety. Fine, doc, whatever. He gave me a tranquilizer and told me to take it whenever I felt what I felt when I was in that room. *OK, you're the guy with the letters after his name,* I thought.

I decided to test out the medication. I went into the studio. It was like entering a sauna of bad news. My heart raced, so I ran out and swallowed a pill. It didn't do much other than knock me out. As a web designer, I sometimes need to stay awake for long periods; taking medicine like that could wind up costing me expensive time. I tossed the bottle almost as soon as I got up.

One day—this was about a month after the old man had passed—I was lying in my bed, staring at the ceiling. Martha was at the foot of the bed, purring softly. I found I couldn't think about that room without thinking of Dad. It was as if the two thoughts were joined by a shackle. When one thought came, the other followed close behind, rattling the chain.

My mind turned to ghosts for the first time. I remembered reading some old folklore about hauntings. It was in one of those book series that you used to be able to order off the TV. All about UFOs and the paranormal. I still had the books in boxes in my closet. I dug them out, found the right volume, and searched until I found what I was looking for.

Animals, it said, had a special sensitivity to ghostly presences. That alone was enough to bring the fear into my collarbone. My heart sped up a bit. I closed my eyes and calmed myself with steady breathing, then opened and continued reading. I finally found the exact passage I'd gone searching for. "Take a cat," it said, "and look between its ears in the direction in which its looking. You'll be able to see what it sees."

You can laugh if you want, but I tried it. I picked Martha up off the bed. She protested with a loud kitty-cat whine. I brought her to the threshold of the studio; I could already smell the aftershave. My heart raced. Martha began to squirm and growl. I held her up, facing the interior of the room. She mewled and squawked and thrashed in my arms until I had to let her go for fear she'd scratch my eyes out. She went scampering away.

After that, I noticed that Martha was avoiding me more and more over the course of the next couple of weeks. It was almost as if I'd emerged from that room that first day with a kind of psychic stink on me, one that got worse with the passage of time.

Then finally, after another week, some good news came in the form of a phone call.   They'd sorted out the red tape and my inheritance was due to arrive any day.

I hung up the phone, went to the threshold of the studio, and looked in.

"You didn't win this one," I said out loud. "I did."

I instantly regretted what had come out of my mouth. I thought of Dad alone in that room, dying. What must have gone through his mind. Loneliness? Despair? Love and loss? My heart started racing again. I moved away from the room and was fine.

Then I realized something. Was this all in my head? There was only one way to find out—the scientific way.

I moved closer to the room and my heart started racing yet again. *It's OK,* I told myself, *just enter. There are no such thing as ghosts.*

I went completely in and was submerged in anxiety. Cold sweat began to bead on my forehead. Things started getting blurry. A had a pain in my chest.

This *is what it was like for Dad*, I thought, as everything was suddenly draped in black.

* * *

I woke up in the hospital.

"You've head a massive heart attack," said a kind-faced doctor. "We performed a quadruple bypass. You should be fine."

I managed to croak out a response. "Who brought me here?"

"I believe it was your landscaper, Cesar. I think he's here now."

"Can I see him?"

Cesar. Good old, wonderful lifesaver. He had been getting a patch of weeds along the base of the house right by my studio window when he saw me hit the floor. He had no cell phone. He rammed in the back door with his shoulder and then dragged me and drove me to the hospital in his truck. I told him I didn't know how to thank him.

"One question," he said to me. He wore a kind of embar-rassed smile.

"What is it?"

"That place. That room in your home? It smelled so nice. Is that your aftershave lotions? What is the name?"

I leaned my head back on the pillow and closed my eyes.

"Sir?"

I giggled, and that giggle turned into a laugh, which morphed slowly into a sob. It was the only thing I could do as I thought of Dad, the heart I inherited from him, and the money he left me that would just about cover my out-of-pocket medical expenses and little else.

Black Sea

I t's so easy to lose yourself at sea. Staring into the vast, emerald ocean, its shiny eyes winked back at me as the light from the golden sun bounced off the still water. There's something majestic about it. At sea, nothing matters. You can leave behind your past and embrace the open water like Leviathan searching for a new home.

That's exactly what I was there to do. Escape my past and set sail on an adventure that could possibly rekindle the fire within me. I won't lie to you: I felt dead inside. When the Mary Harper 3 was boarded with beautiful people from this wretched city of San Francisco, my only hope was to cut ties with everything that reminded me of him.

This is kind of uncomfortable to talk about, even with a psychologist like you, but since I have no choice I'll explain my reason for completely uprooting my life and quitting my corporate job for the position as a rookie hostess on the cruise line.

My husband of twenty-six years, Robert, turned out to be the biggest mistake of my life. There were many rumors over the years, but I ignored them or shut them down before they opened my eyes to the truth. We lost many friends over the years and people looked down on me for being married to such a disgusting man. I don't blame them. I just … I just couldn't accept his adulterous ways. I trusted him with all my heart, or at least, I wanted to trust him.

When I was younger, I had the opportunity to travel to Paris and study art. It was my dream for many years but Eric convinced me to stay in San Francisco and pursue a job in accounting with him. He proposed, and of course, I said yes.

It was heartbreaking to learn that he had cheated on me more times than I would like to count. Heck, even people I considered friends betrayed me along with him. I wasted twenty-six years of my life married to that cheating bastard. All I am now is a forty-year-old woman with no children and a cheating soon-to-be-ex-husband.

I had to get away from that life. It was tearing me apart.

So, when I came across the position in a local newspaper, I impulsively decided to quit my job, sell most of my stuff, and set sail on this ship to a brand new world. It was a good start and that spark in me was definitely being reignited. My nerves were soothed by the change in scenery and my mind was just a bit too occupied with guests to focus on my problems.

Things spiraled out of control when I found myself wheeling desserts down the aisles to those guests who opted to order in. I was greeted by a cute old couple who lightly bickered with each other and for a second I admired them before the pain of my old memories kick-started the dreadful depression coursing through my veins.

I shrugged it off and moved on to room 161 where I met an Arab man with a neatly shaped beard that coated his jawline dressed in a white garment that looked a lot like a dress. His head was covered by a hat and a sweet fragrance emanated from him. As he smiled and gestured for his chocolate mousse, his black eyes gradually shifted back to mine and a curious look settled on his face. With an unusual accent he said, "It still hurts."

"Pardon?" I asked.

"I can see you've suffered a great ordeal in your life. This is no place for someone like you. The sea is known to be the home to a completely different world," he warned. I felt incredibly anxious and afraid in that moment.

How could he tell I was in pain?

I did my best to wear a shielded face that revealed nothing of what I felt inside and yet this stranger looked and spoke as if he could see into my soul. I brushed it off with a smile and passed over his order before turning around and wheeling my way back to the main cabin. I could sense that he was watching me and as I made my way to the end of the corridor, I glanced back quickly to find him standing dreadfully still, just watching me with a deadly stare.

As I made my way to the main cabin, I could hear distant voices chanting in the background. I assumed that it would be a few vacationers just engaging in some playful banter in the restroom but when I peeked inside, it was absolutely empty and the sound stopped too. I made my way to a basin and flung the handle up, causing a stream of water to gush out.

Splashing some cold water onto my face, I stared into the mirror, looking back at the crusty old crows feet that grew around the corners of my blue eyes. Having blonde hair didn't help shield my age, especially as it had faded quite significantly through the years.

When did I become so old? I thought.

Just as I dropped my head down to take another swing at the cold water, I was completely disgusted to find thick, green slime oozing out of the tap and on to my hands. I jerked back in disgust, holding my hands in front of me. The gooey green substance clung to my fingers like glue and as I tried to shake it off, it grew tighter on my skin.

It wouldn't budge, and it squeezed against my skin making me feel incredibly uncomfortable. Within a few short seconds I felt the circulation to my hands cutting off and they grew numb. Arthritic pain coursed through my wrists and my hairs stood on end.

Just as I bolted out of the restroom screaming for help, Mike, the manager, came racing towards me to render some assistance. I flung my hands up to show him what happened but when I looked again, there was nothing on them.

He asked me what had happened and I explained to him that there was some substance gushing out of the tap but when we entered the restroom again, we found nothing. I couldn't explain it and Mike looked at me questionably. Perhaps he thought I was a crazy old hag. Hell, that's how I felt.

We parted ways and he told me to head upstairs to the main deck to clear up the mess from the party earlier that night. I nodded and continued walking upstairs. I couldn't explain what had just happened.

Perhaps I was too drained out or hallucinating from the pills I took to ease my seasickness. Nevertheless, the smell of old fish lingered in the air and the confusion of what happened earlier kept me on edge.

Just as I found my way, reaching the door at the apex of the staircase, I could hear those distinct voices again. I stopped in hopes of catching what was being said but it sounded like a group of men speaking in a different language. I couldn't quite make out the words, but in a fit of irritation I flung open the red metal door, hoping to be exposed to a group of men having a good laugh; all I found was an empty deck with liquor bottles and paper plates scattered around the place. It was going to be a long night. I had expected this to be a new start and a new adventure but it was merely shaping up to be a big nightmare.

Did I really leave my comfortable office for this?

Weird strangers, weird substances that disappeared, and voices that came and went. Something was wrong with me. It was just a bit after noon and I spent at least an hour cleaning up the place with Maggie and Jill—twins who worked on this ship until their gap year was over. They were sweet little brunettes, at least when no one was supervising. I stood near the helm and propped myself against the railing to look at the stars. Sure, it may have been a weird night, but things would get better now. The worst was over.

Just as I turned around, I felt a cold sensation run down my neck that gave me chills up my spine. I spun around to find the Arab man right behind me wearing a devious smile and Maggie and Jill nowhere in sight.

He lunged out, wrapping his hands around my neck and squeezing with all his might. I tried to scream but my pipes were being smashed tight from the sheer force of his grip.

I tried punching at his hands and kicking him but it made no difference. This monstrous man was far too strong and the lack of oxygen made me panic and squirm around like dying prey. Blood rushed to my eyes and head and the rest of my body felt limp. I remember grasping at his face, trying to dig my fingers into his eyes, but everything faded to black before I could.

In that moment, the last thought that entered my head before passing out was of Robert. As I slowly regained consciousness, I found myself lying on the cold, wet deck. Thoughts flowed into my brain very slowly and everything around me seemed to be in a haze. I wiped my eyes and grabbed on to the handle bar next to me.

Pulling myself up, I was greeted by the most horrendous sight I had ever seen in my entire life. A group of naked, bloodied, and butchered men with pus oozing from their wounded heads stood around me in a semi-circle. They were chanting what sounded like Arabic words and they stared back at me with cold, white eyes. I screamed as loud as I could even though pain coursed through my neck and throat.

At the center of this group was the man who throttled me but this time he, too, was naked and battered.

His insides were hanging out and around his neck was a steel chain. He walked up to me and somehow my body became stiff. I tried to scream but no sound escaped my lips. I couldn't even turn my head or blink. My eyes began to burn and the fear that riddled my body was far too overwhelming. He leaned his foul-smelling mouth to my ear and whispered, "Your weak soul is perfect for our Lord. Jump!" Before I knew it, my body began to move on its own.

I didn't know what to do.

It was as if something was controlling my body and I was just a backseat driver who had no control. I felt my hands grip the bar behind me and as tears ran down my face, I watched as the men held hands and their chant grew louder. The last thing I remember was my back against the railing and my legs pushing off the ground.

I fell backwards over the railing and my stiff body hit the icy water. I woke up the next morning in the medical bay. My body was bruised and sore from head to toe and there were bandages around my chest and wrists.

The nurse paid me a visit and when I asked her what had happened and told her about the men who did this to me, she told me to calm down and that the captain would be down to see me. He came to see me, alright. More than anything he was upset and pissed that my actions would tarnish the good reputation of the cruise line. I tried telling him about the men but what he said shocked the living daylights out of me.

There were no men on the deck that night and neither was there an Arab man in room 161. In fact, there was no one booked into 161.

Turns out the twins somehow watched me throw myself overboard; no one else was on the deck.

They heard me screaming but I apparently was too dazed to even notice them. And that's why I'm here now, talking to you, Dr. Mike. I swear to God I didn't try to kill myself and I'm not crazy. Something tried to kill me that night and I saw those men. I don't need a psychologist.

They were real.

I swear, they were real!

Call from a Future Soul

I was working late at the library one night when it first happened. Now, I know what you're thinking: library, old books, the desolation and silence—that opening scene from *Ghostbusters*?

Not exactly.

There weren't any six-foot stacks of books in the aisles. No glowing old ladies who turned into demons. No ectoplasm. Nothing of the sort.

No, the library wasn't haunted. I was. I wish my ex-husband were alive so you could ask him. He was a lot of things, my ex. But he wasn't a liar. I know that now. I didn't know it then.

I'll tell you how it starts. It starts with the smell of seaweed. It ends with a child's laughter.

Let me start by saying that we were one of those happy couples that everybody hates. You know what I mean, one of those couples that kinda makes you sick to look at them. Public displays of affection, giggling at private jokes, playing footsie under the table— totally annoying.

"Don't have a kid," they all said. By "they," I mean our married friends with children. "Everything changes," they said, and we believed them. We saw them with our young, objective eyes. Yes, they'd changed. They were once like us. They were young and vibrant with the world ahead of them. Then the kid arrived, and everything was harried and tired. All was eternal vigilance with them, never any time for friends, and they had no time to themselves—or for each other.

We'd resolved it: that definitely wasn't going to happen us.

Well, I don't need to tell you how it goes. Nature works by her own rules. We got pregnant.

Guess what? *Nothing changed.*

Strange, right?

We were still the same googly-eyed lovebirds who could make you throw up. Our child, little Alex, he was the light of our life, the perfect product of our union.

I was a stay-at-home mom for a while, but it eventually came time to go back to work. I had to work, but I also *wanted* to work. Steven was OK with that. He was a very modern husband.

So it was during this time that I had my first experience. I was working one night at the library. It was a Tuesday night and it was dead, as usual. I swear I saw tumbleweed blowing past me.

Now let me just say that libraries have a special smell to them. Those who love books, who snuggle with books, know what I mean. Especially small libraries like the one I work in. The smell of actual, physical books is a wonderful perfume. You should try it sometime. Crack one open and sniff the spine. I love my Kindle, but I'm telling you, you can't get that smell with an eBook.

As I said, it's one of the pleasures of working in a library. And you're always aware of it.

But this night, that smell was replaced by another smell. It's hard to describe it. It was a wet smell, almost like a swamp. But it wasn't dank or rotten, it was just … *wet.*

Ever get up close to a fish tank?

So I did what anyone would do: I looked around. I was the only one there. I thought maybe there was some sewage leak. But it wasn't a sewage smell. Still, certain minds try to formulate the most rational explanations.

The smell went away as quickly as it had come. I checked around the building. There were no windows open. The AC system was up to date, but maybe it was something having to do with that. Only the AC wasn't on. The vents weren't even open. They click open when the AC comes on. You can hear them do it, especially when you're all alone in an empty building.

OK, fine, I thought. *Some fluke thing. Don't worry about it.* Steven texted me, telling me Alex was giving him a problem with bedtime. Alex was two and starting to earn the "terrible" adjective that usually accompanies that number.

When I read that text, the smell came back. It was heavier now, and I started to feel woozy. I was having trouble breathing.

The air became thick like syrup. And my vision was blurry. As I gasped, I tasted this horrible chicken soup-like quality to the air. It made me sick.

Then it was over. The air was clear. I could breathe again. And I was on the floor. I'd dropped my phone.

I quickly dialed Steven.

He answered with a whisper. "He just fell asleep." He sounded haggard, like he'd been through some terrible ordeal. Alex must have really given him the business.

"Steven," I said, "I'm not well."

"That's funny," he said. "I'm not feeling well either."

"You don't understand. I'm really not feeling well at all. There's a leak or something in this place. I keep smelling it and it's making me sick."

"What are you smelling?"

"I can't explain it. Water tinged with algae?"

There was silence.

"Steven?"

"Do you suppose maybe we ate something weird?"

"Why do you say that?"

"Never mind," he said, "That wouldn't be giving us both olfactory hallucinations."

"What?"

"I'm smelling it too," he said.

"Steven, I'm scared."

"It has to be something we ate. That Chinese food last night. I thought it tasted off."

"But how could food poisoning give us—what did you call it? Olfactory hallucinations?"

"I don't know. But if you have a better explanation, I'd like to hear it."

"There could be some kind of gas leak in the neighborhood."

"I just talked to Larry next door. He sounded fine. I could call someone else?"

"No," I said. "We're closing soon. I'll be home and we'll see."

When I got home, he was pale.

"What's wrong?"

"It was overwhelming," he said; he sounded winded. "That smell. I was suffocating in it."

It was too late to call anyone. So we did what any young couple would do: we searched the Internet.

After turning up page after page of unsatisfactory explanations—mostly involving things we'd already considered—we chanced upon some blogger who proposed a far-fetched, yet, I have to say, interesting theory.

The future can call back to us, they said. *And why is that? The answer is actually very simple: human bodies may be bound by the rules of linear time, but human souls are not. They are the voices we hear at night. And their essence can come on a breeze.*

So, according to this person, both Steven's and my experiences were some future soul calling back to us?

No. There was a better explanation out there somewhere.

But I'd had enough. I couldn't be bothered. The experience had tired me out. Steven was exhausted from dealing with a stubborn two-year-old. It was bedtime. The next day was a Saturday and we'd promised ourselves a family day out.

It's difficult for me to talk about this next part. This is the first time I've ever set it down. I can't remember it without reliving it, so you'll have to bear with me. All I can do is to recall it in snapshots.

I see the cruel forces of fate that brought us to the crowded park that day. It was crowded. We left and opted for the beach instead.

The next snapshot I see is little Alex running through the sand.

My memory is so foggy that I don't even know how it began between Steven and me, but I do know that at some point I was looking in the bag that was supposed to be holding the sunscreen.

I don't know what happened first. All I know is that we were arguing over who was supposed to have packed it. He said it was me. I said it was him. There was a lot of frustration, a lot of anger that had pent up over the course of our relationship. True love requires emotional honesty. I know that now. I didn't know it then.

We'd been kidding ourselves that it was all perfect, all lovey-dovey, cooing all the time. True love—for a child—demands a sacrifice of some of that selfishness.

And here the snapshots continue. There are accusations and name-calling. Some of it very personal.

Each one accuses the other of being neglectful. All because of sunscreen.

We don't yet know the real meaning of neglectful.

I hear the waves crashing.

I smell the seaweed.

I look up. Alex is gone.

Panic. A frantic search.

His little hat comes washing in on a foamy wave.

* * *

My dear reader, the human mind will do anything with to cope with guilt. For Steven, that meant a search for answers that led us to our darkest place in the months following our tragedy.

It began when Steven mentioned the blog article we'd seen that night. He reminded me about what he called "our shared hallucinations" of salt water and suffocation.

"Do you remember what that article said?"

"I don't remember exactly. I thought it was all a little ridiculous."

"It said that sometimes we can hear the voices of souls from the future. Remember what we felt that night? That was no shared hallucination. It was Alex's soul coming back to warn us. He was just a baby and didn't know how to say it, so he said it as best as he could by making us experience a physical picture of his death."

I couldn't deal with that. We were trying to rebuild our shattered lives and here my husband was bringing us down to wallow in our guilt.

I was crying now, trying to catch the grief that was coming out of me, trying to reel it in so that I could speak. Finally, I caught my breath.

"Steven, listen to me. We're both crushed with guilt over our neglect of Alex. And you're trying to rationalize it by saying we should have known because Alex was trying to warn us from the future? Come back to earth, Steven. Nothing can make sense out of that tragedy. And Alex's death is on both of our hands!"

Any relationship that has been struck by heartbreaking tragedy will either survive bound by the common experience or crumble to dust. There's no in-between. We crumbled.

We eventually separated, then divorced.

I threw myself into my work as best as I could. But then I got the call. After that I was never the same. I was at home when it happened.

"You—" he used a word that I hated. "You did this to me. You let him die and now this is happening."

He was hyperventilating.

"Steven," I said. "Enough already!"

He gurgled threw his tears. "Remember how I used to carry my baby on my back in that sling? Remember?"

I started to cry. "I remember."

"Well," he said, allowing his sob to subside, "I can't ... I ... *I felt his breath on my neck.*" There was a long pause as we both waited for the other to speak.

He hung up after that.

The next day, I found out Steven had killed himself.

It was a tortuous week. I was the last one he'd spoken to. He'd referenced me in a suicide note, admitting that he at least shared in the responsibility for Alex's death, and now he could finally rest; now I would now have to shoulder the guilt alone.

His funeral was a modest affair. I don't remember much of it. I remember the faces of those who care enough to wish me well, but mostly I was a pariah. Steven's family ignored me. Our friends were awkward.

And then I was alone before the grave. They'd at least given me the respect of allowing me my solitude with Steven.

I told him I was sorry. And I told him that he was now with our little boy whose grave was right next to him. Alex forgave us now.

But forgiveness doesn't come that easily, I guess. Because there was the smell again. It came with a soft breeze. It got warmer. And the taste of salt hit my tongue. And with this, a new sensation: my ears rang with a sound like a tiny tinkling bell.

I recognized it for what it was, plain as any sound I'd ever heard, as real as anything you could touch. I knew this sound.

It was right behind my ears.

It was my child's laughter.

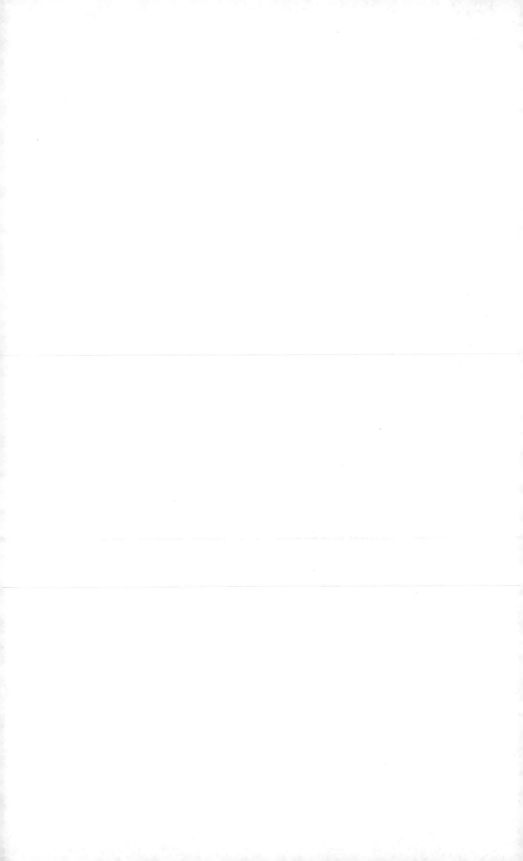

Bonus for readers of this book

Get 3 FREE ghost stories at
www.paranormalpublishing.com/ghoststories

If you enjoyed reading this book, please consider leaving
a positive review on Amazon so others might find it. If there
was something you believe needed changing or you didn't like,
please email the publisher with your comments at
Publisher@paranormalpublishing.net

Additional books of interest from

Paranormal Publishing

available on Amazon and at

www.PararnormalPublishing.net

Volumes I, II, III: *True Ghost Stories and Hauntings*

More stories about ghosts and hauntings from Simon B. Murik.

Boxed set of Volumes I, II, and III

For kids: *Ghost Coloring Book*
Kids love coloring these ghosts as they bring
them to life. Let your imagination fly and have
lots of fun with this spooky activity book!

Made in the USA
San Bernardino, CA
12 June 2016